# FRIENDS

## Gloria Whelan

# FRIENDS

## Gloria Whelan

Thunder Bay Press

Published by Thunder Bay Press
Publisher: Sam Speigel
Designed and typeset by Maureen MacLaughlin-Morris
Artwork and cover by Jenifer Thomas

ISBN: 1-882376-55-2 hardcover
      1-882376-54-4 trade

Printed in the United States of America

97 98 99 2000   1 2 3 4 5 6 7 8 9

For all the little "Couzens."

## CHAPTER 1

The southern Michigan winters are warm as a kitchen one day and cold as sheets the next. One day the snow comes feathering in from Lake Michigan. The next day soft breezes steal up from the south. And people come from the south. Secretly. Two years ago my friend, Martha Crosswhite, her mother and father and her sisters and brothers arrived here in Marshall from the south. From Kentucky. Slaves.

After I came to know her Martha Crosswhite told me, "Our master in Kentucky was going to break us apart. Mama and some of us children sent one place, Papa and the rest of us, another. Forever. So we ran away."

"Why did you come to Marshall?" I asked.

"We heard slaves like us come here and got themselves a handshake. No bird travels faster than happy news."

It is true. Marshall is a welcoming town. And proud. All three thousand of us. In 1837, just ten years ago, Michigan was declared a state. Marshall hopes to be the capitol. Some people are so sure of it they are building a big house for the governor to live in. And something else. The new Michigan Central railroad comes through our town.

Martha says the railroad is important, "If a slave don't want to settle down when they land here they get on the train and head for Detroit. There's places there. They put you in a hidey-hole. Next day they sit you in a boat and row you away to Canada and you're free forever."

Martha and her family live on the east side of town. There must be fifty Negroes who live there. Many of them, like the Crosswhites, came up from the south as slaves. They settled in and got jobs and built themselves houses like Mr. Crosswhite did. They have a watchful, over-the-shoulder look. Any day their owner could come up from the south and take them back. Lydia says, "Over my dead body."

I met Martha because of Lydia who is my stepmother. My mother died of influenza a year after I was born. My father and a housekeeper took care of me until just two years ago when Papa married Lydia. Lydia was a school teacher. After she got married to Papa she had to give up her job because the school board doesn't allow married teachers. "Can't do two things at once," they said. They don't know Lydia.

# FRIENDS

Papa says she's a tornado. She is the first to greet slaves who have escaped to Marshall. The other Negroes take them in. Lydia brings clothing and extra food. I often go with her. It makes me shiver just to see how little they have to wear when they come north and how thin they are with hunger.

I listen to Lydia gently question them to discover what they can do. Maybe blacksmithing or carpentry or farm work. In the south they weren't allowed to go to school. Lydia sets about finding them a job, even if it means bullying one of Papa's friends into hiring them.

There are some in town like the lawyer, Mr. Lurfert, who say Lydia is breaking the law to help runaway slaves. They call her an abolitionist. That's a fancy name for someone who is against slavery. Lydia doesn't care what she is called. She says, "The Lord meant human beings to be free." Then she sticks more pins in her pile of red hair that is always coming loose. Like she was caught in a whirlwind. She puts on heavy boots against the snow and mud and out she goes with me trailing after. Like as not she brings some sick or hungry person back with us. The hungry ones she feeds until all that's left for our own supper is porridge.

The sick ones she lines up on the chairs in Papa's clinic. Papa is a doctor. He complains. "Lydia, there is hardly enough time in the day to see all my own patients. How can I find time for your waifs?" But when she looks woeful he shakes his head and only says, "Well, my dear, I can't scold a kind heart."

It was how I met Martha Crosswhite. Last summer Lydia brought Mrs. Crosswhite to see Papa because her new baby was sick. Its cough was like a bark and scratchy. Martha came along. She was ten years old, just my age. She had soft brown eyes and velvety brown skin and her hair was in tight little braids, a ribbon on the end of every single one. While Papa saw Mrs. Crosswhite and her baby, Lydia fixed Martha and me cocoa and shortbread. Martha drank the cocoa slowly. She grinned at me over her cup. "Guess I'll make it last a long time," she said. Half her shortbread she slipped in her pocket. "My brothers and sister have to taste this."

Lydia asked Martha how her family got to Marshall. "When my daddy heard our master, Mr. Giltner, was going to sell a part of us, he said we had to go away fast. They might send us south. You got to work in the rice fields there. That's wet work. Your feet just about rot. Or the cotton fields. From first light to the sun go down feeding the cotton gin. And the overseers watch you sharp-eyed. They got switches that sting.

"Daddy got us a little boat. He hid it in the weeds like the woman of Levi hid baby Moses. One night we got in the boat. If we all hold our breath we just fit. The water was right up to the top of the boat and couldn't wait to get in to us. Daddy pushed the boat with a big pole. Some places the pole didn't even touch bottom. That boat spun around one way and then another. Just like a wash tub. We thought, 'Now we're going to the bottom of the river for sure!' But the little boat got us across. We were out of Kentucky and in Indiana. We didn't want to say goodbye to that boat. It was such a good friend to us.

"We traveled by night. The north star never out of our sight. Cloudy nights we felt which side of the trees the moss grew. We slept in fields. We slept in haystacks with the straw poking us everywhere. We ate what we could get our hands on. We dug up carrots left in the fields. We ate cabbage. Raw. We were out in the rain two days and wet clear through. Some Quakers took us in. They wore funny clothes but they set us in front of the fire and dried us off and fed us. Then there was a loud knocking on the door. It sounded like bad news to us.

"The Quaker ladies pushed us down a trap door under their floor. They got out their sewing and when the slave catchers come in they say they just a sewing club and was there something wrong with that? When the slave catchers were gone they pulled us out and told us where to go next. And what you think? All those clothes they sewed. They handed them over to us.

"The next night we had to run. Daddy and Mama got separated. I was with Mama. We thought never to see Daddy again. It was a week before we found each other. We held hands and never let go again. Then we got to Marshall and people told us, 'Stay here.' So we did."

## CHAPTER 2

I had never heard a story like Martha's. I didn't breathe through the whole telling of it. I longed to hear it all over again so a couple of days later I went to the Crosswhite house and called for Martha. It was a hot July day. In the backyards hollyhocks and morning glories drooped in the heat. The bugs in the trees were screaming. The air was so damp it was hard to breathe in and out. My starched petticoat pricked and jabbed. My long stockings felt clammy. I could feel sweat running down my back. When Martha came to the door I asked, "You want to go put your feet in the river?"

The Kalamazoo River flows right down to the middle of Marshall. The nice thing about the river, it stays cold even in summer. A river is too busy to let the sun warm it. We took our shoes and stockings off and stuck our feet in the cold water. Martha said, "I can feel the coolness work itself up all the way from my toes to the top of my head." She watched the river like she could see as far as its beginning and its end. "You could make yourself a raft," she said. "It could carry you away fast as anything. Nobody catch you." Just beyond the town the river backs up into the mill pond. We swim there in the summer and skate there in winter. "Have you got a swimming dress," I asked.

Martha stared at me. "A dress just for swimming?"

Lydia made her one. It was just like mine, cotton jersey, with long sleeves and a skirt half way down to our ankles with trousers underneath. Martha wouldn't get hers wet until she saw me jump in. We made a raft just like Martha said and floated down the river and then ran along the river's edge pulling the raft back again with a rope. The raft scattered the ducks like blowing leaves and sent the muskrats into their humpy houses. We played runaway slaves. We always escaped.

All summer long we explored the town. I was surprised at how little of the town Martha had seen. She said, "In Kentucky we keep to ourselves."

"This isn't Kentucky," I told her. At the blacksmith shop we watched sparks from the anvil rise up like fireflies. We watched them make piney smelling boards at the lumber mill.

When fall came, long lines of wagons heaped with bags of grain made their way to the stone mills. We looked on as the mills turned the wheat into flour. At the coopers we saw them make barrels to ship the flour.

We collected leaves from every kind of tree in town: walnut, catalpa, sycamore, maple, beech, cottonwood, oak, and elm. We pressed them under books and pasted them into a notebook and wrote down their names. The front of my book said, "Trees in Marshall." On the front of her book Martha printed, "Trees in my Town."

Sometimes we stopped at the lending library. Until we got chased away we stood around reading the novels. They told about poor working girls who became princesses. "I don't think there are enough princes to go around," Martha said. Lydia had some novels at home but she kept them hidden. A lot of people in town said novels were bad. They said you could get addicted to them.

What we liked to do best was to look in shop windows. The dry goods store had bolts of cloth: flannel, silk, calico, lawn, and a muslin printed all over with flowers. "It would be summer every time you'd wear that dress," Martha said. There were bakeries and shoemakers and tailors and jewelry stores. Our favorite was the millinery store. We loved to look at the hats in the window. Martha pointed to her favorite hat. "That's got so many feathers it's going to fly away." My favorite hat had pink ribbons and a rose as big as a cabbage.

# FRIENDS

Sometimes we just sat on one of the benches in the town square. Across from the square was Marshall House, one of the finest hotels in the whole state. It was made of real bricks instead of wood. It had forty rooms to it.

We liked to watch the stagecoaches pull up with well-dressed travelers. Isaac Jacobs would hand the people out of the coach and take their trunks. Mr. Jacobs was the hostler at Marshall House and wore a uniform with brass buttons.

The travelers were mostly men come to do business in town. In a day or so we would see them get in the stagecoach and leave.

Sometimes we would follow them to the railroad station. The train would come roaring through like a hungry lion. The men would go east to Detroit. Or west to Battle Creek.

From Jackson they could take a stagecoach to Chicago. Martha would look sad at their going, "I'm not going to leave this town," she said, "ever."

I went with Martha's mother and her brothers and sisters to the woods to pick berries. Martha's mother was a large soft woman. But quiet. One of the children always seemed to be burrowing into her softness. Lydia was skinny and I don't remember my mother. Mrs. Crosswhite was quiet. She seemed always to be thinking of something she couldn't say.

# FRIENDS

We picked wild strawberries in June. They were tucked under the grasses. We got down on our hands and knees to see them. We were eye to eye with the beetles. You had to be careful not to squeeze the tiny berries. "Nothing left of them," Martha laughed, "but the juice on your fingers."

Blueberries were easier to gather. Pails full. In July there were wild raspberries, seedy but their taste was like summer. In August we picked blackberries The briars left scratches on our legs and arms. "Like a wildcat got us," Martha said. The Crosswhites couldn't get enough of the berries. Martha said, "In Kentucky we pick from light to dark but all the berries went to the master. All the land belong to him. 'Til we got here I didn't think anything was left over for us."

## CHAPTER 3

By the time we got the last blackberries fall had come. It was time to go back to school. Martha went to the district school. I went to one of Marshall's small private schools. At our school we learned grammar, history, rhetoric, geography, deportment and needle-work. Lots of needlework. In first grade I started out by making a needle case. In second grade it was an apron. In third grade, drawers. In fourth grade a petti-coat. This year I was making a blouse. Miss Growl-ing, whose school it was, said, "Hilda, as usual you're not paying attention to what you are doing. You've put your sleeves in backwards. You'll have to take them home and rip them out." I sighed. I hate ripping out. It's like the train when it backs up. It's not get-ting anywhere.

Martha was watching me take out the stitches. I told her, "You're lucky you don't go to Miss Growling's school. Your fingers would be all needle pricks."

"You're supposed to use a thimble," Martha said.

"I know but I have to feel what I'm doing. Anyhow, it isn't just the needlework. Miss Growling makes us practice being polite and even curtsying. She's tall and boney. When she bends down to show us how to curtsy she looks like a grasshopper."

I was showing Martha how to curtsy when she said, "No point in my learning. I couldn't go to your school even if my daddy could pay the tuition."

"Why not?"

"I'm not the right color. It's just for white girls."

For some reason what Martha said made me angry and I snapped, "I don't believe you."

"You ask," Martha said. "There's a lot you don't know. Not everything is fair in Marshall." And she flounced angrily out of the house.

The next morning when Miss Growling was pointing out the puckers in my armholes I said, "I've got a friend who might want to come here to school, Miss Growling."

She smiled and stopped criticizing my sewing. Every pupil she got meant more money for her. "That would be very nice, dear. I'm sure she would be welcome here. What is her name?"

"Martha Crosswhite."

"I don't believe I know the Crosswhite family. What does her father do?"

"He's a carpenter. It's a Negro family."

Mrs. Growling's eyebrows shot up. "We don't have Negro children in this school, Hilda. Surely you know that."

"Why not?" I was truly puzzled.

"I'm surprised you ask, Hilda. I am sure your parents would not want you associating with Negro children."

"I associate with Martha all the time."

Miss Growling looked like she had swallowed a thistle. She bent over the sleeves in my blouse saying in a sort of raspy voice, "You'll have to rip them out again, Hilda."

That afternoon Miss Growling came to visit. When Lydia caught sight of her marching up our walk she groaned. But Lydia was all politeness when she went to the door. "How nice of you to pay us a call," Lydia said. "Let me get you a cup of tea."

Miss Growling perched on the edge of a chair, her knees sticking up in two points under her skirt. Her sharp elbows aiming right and left. "That's very kind of you, Mrs. Lovett, but I take no stimulants."

"I hope Hilda isn't giving you any trouble," Lydia said, trying to guess why Miss Growling was there. "I know she can be a little impetuous at times."

"I'm afraid it is more serious than that. I wonder if I could speak with you alone?"

# FRIENDS

Lydia gave me a worried look. "Hilda, I didn't have time to make bread today. Could you run out to the bakery and bring me home a loaf?"

I took as much time as I could to put on my coat and hat but there was nothing but silence to hear in the sitting room. On the way back from the bakery I saw Papa's carriage. Papa was coming from a house call and gave me a ride. In his tall hat and dark coat and black bag Papa always looks very serious to me. Not like the Papa I'm used to.

On our way home lots of people called out to Papa and waved to him. They like him in town not just because he's a doctor but because he's their doctor. Lydia said, "They don't just respect you, Emery, they like you."

The moment we walked in the door Lydia was at us. "Emery, that odious, priggish, high-handed Miss Growling was here this afternoon!" Lydia's red hair was flying every which way.

Papa always made a point of being especially calm when Lydia was excited about something. Sort of like a teeter-totter. He took off his coat and carefully hung it up before he asked, "I hope Hilda is behaving."

"It isn't Hilda, it's us. Miss Growling said she was surprised and disappointed that we would let Hilda associate with a Negro child! Disappointed! Did you ever hear anything so bigoted and narrow-minded? I won't have Hilda spending another day in that school."

"Now, Lydia, let's not be hasty. We can't just pull Hilda out of school without giving it some thought."

"I have been thinking for the last hour, Emery."

"Yes, but you have only been thinking one thing, my dear. Hilda's tuition is paid up to the end of the month."

"If it is a question of money, Emery, I will sell my pearl earrings."

"Lydia!" Papa looked truly shocked. "You are talking nonsense."

"Papa," I said, "You always say I shouldn't be rude and question what my teacher tells me. Do you want me to question what Miss Growling says about Martha?"

Papa stared at me for a long minute. "Yes, I do."

"Well, if I question that, how will I know I shouldn't question other things she tells me?"

Lydia and Papa exchanged a long look. "You win, Lydia," Papa said. "I'll write to Miss Growling and Hilda can start the district school next week."

I had not seen Martha since she had flounced out of our house. On Monday morning when I walked into her class at the district school she stared and stared at me. The teacher introduced me to the class.

"This is Hilda Lovett, students. She is joining our

class. I am sure you will all make her welcome."

As soon as the teacher's back was turned I passed a note to Martha. It said, "It's getting fairer in Marshall!"

Martha just grinned.

After school we walked home together. We were looking in the window of the dry goods store at some lace, fine as spider webs, when Miss Growling walked by. When she saw us she stuck her nose in the air.

## CHAPTER 4

The trouble began on a gray winter day when the wet snow was like a cold drop of rain on your cheek. When I called for Martha I saw a white man coming out of her house. I had never seen him before. He was a short man with small eyes and a pointed nose. He looked like a hungry possum or rat searching out a morsel of food. "Who was that?" I asked Martha.

"He said he was from the census. He asked who are we? He took all our names from Mama."

Martha and I waited for him to go to the rest of the houses and ask his questions. He never did. He just started walking toward town. Martha shook her head. "Why just us?" She whispered the question although the man was nearly a block away from us.

I caught Martha's fear like it was measles. "Let's follow him," I was whispering, too.

Martha hung back. "Come on." I pulled on her arm.

The snow was all rain now. Our caps and mittens were soaked and smelled like wet dog. The man was hurrying. Once he looked around as if someone might be watching him. All he saw was us. He gave us no more mind than a couple of sparrows on a tree. We followed him to the town square and Marshall House.

As he walked up to the hotel two men hurried out to meet the man. One was well dressed with a tall beaver hat and a velvet collar to his coat. The other man had a corduroy jacket and a cap. They weren't dressed for a winter day. Their clothes were for a warmer place.

When she saw them Martha gasped as if all the breath had been squeezed out of her. In a frightened whisper she said, "I know those men."

She turned and ran as fast as she could. It took me a long time to catch her. She would only stop for a second. All the time she was looking back toward town.

I held on to her. "Who are they?"

"That one man. He's kin to our first master. That other man. He's kin to the master we run from. They after us for sure. I have to tell my daddy." She pulled away from me. The next minute she was gone.

It was nearly dark when I got home. There was a carriage outside. In the dining room the silver candle holders were lit. I remembered Lydia had warned me to be home early. Mr. Lurfert, who is an important lawyer in town, was coming to dinner.

# FRIENDS

Lydia met me at the door. Before I could tell her what had happened she sent me to clean up.

As I hurried into the dining room she hastily did the top button on my dress and retied the lopsided bow on my sash. Papa and Mr. Lurfert were already seated at the table.

Mr. Lurfert is not exactly fat but his suits always appear as stuffed as a Thanksgiving turkey. The most interesting thing about him is his mustache which looks like someone drew it on his face with a ruler and black ink.

Our good Haviland china and the silver teaspoons were on the table. The dinner would be a tasty one, for Mr. Lurfert was not easy to please. Lydia would have tried hard. He frowned at me as I scraped the floor pulling out my chair.

I knew I should be quiet for Mr. Lurfert did not think children had anything to say worth listening to. But I couldn't hold my tongue. I never can. We had hardly unfolded our hands after grace when I said, "We've got to do something. Guess who Martha and I saw today?"

Mr. Lurfert was frowning. Papa's mouth was opening. Two signals to hush but I couldn't stop myself. "There was a white man who was at the Crosswhite's house asking questions and he wasn't from the census like he said because he didn't go to any other house." I took a breath. Just a quick one. "So we followed him to town and he met these two men at the hotel. Martha said they were related to her masters. She ran home."

Papa forgot to scold me. Instead he asked, "One had a jacket with a velvet collar the other one had a brown corduroy jacket?" He was frowning

"Yes! Yes, that's them!"

Papa was quiet for a minute. "They have been in town for a couple of days. The one man has talked of settling here in Marshall. But I've seen him in the deputy sheriff's office." Papa gave Lydia a worried look.

She looked right back. "Slave catchers!"

A chill went down my spine. I knew what slave catchers were. They were agents of the owners of escaped slaves. They were paid to bring the slaves back. I jumped from my chair.

"Where do you think you are going, young lady?" Papa asked.

"I have to go to the Crosswhites!"

"You will do nothing of the kind. You will finish your supper and then Lydia and I will decide what ought to be done."

I sat back down but they might as well have put a dish of dead mice and snakes in front of me. I couldn't eat a bite.

"I dare say those men are within their rights," Mr.

Lurfert said. "The Fugitive Slave Law of 1793 is clear enough. A slave must be returned to his lawful owner."

"Mr. Lurfert," Lydia said, her eyes flashing, "Kentucky may be a slave state, but Michigan is a free state. In a free state everyone is presumed to be free."

Mr. Lurfert put down his knife and fork. "That may be what you wish, my dear, but it is not the law of the land. The newspapers of this town, both the *Expounder* and the *Statesman* have been irresponsible in writing their anti-slavery propaganda. Not only that. There are people in this town whom I believe to be members of the Michigan Anti-Slavery Society." He looked hard at Lydia who blushed. "Slaves must be returned. That is the law and we are a lawful country." He took up his knife and fork again.

"That's not fair," I shouted.

"Hilda," Papa said in an angry voice. Even Lydia looked shocked.

Mr. Lurfert finished chewing and swallowing and then turned to me. "If everyone did just as they wished, young lady, with no regard for the law, it would not be a pleasant world."

"It will not be pleasant for Martha's family if they have to go back to being slaves and get separated and never see each other again!"

Papa threw his napkin onto the table and stood up. He is a tall man and when he is angry he looks

FRIENDS

even taller. "That is enough, Hilda. Mr. Lurfert is a guest in our house and I will not have him sassed. You go up to your room."

I took a long time and made a lot of noise going up the stairs. Once in my room I knelt down on the floor. There is a hot air register in my bedroom which is just above the dining room. By putting my ear to the grill I could hear everything my parents and Mr. Lurfert said. Papa was talking, "I must apologize for Hilda, Milton. Martha Crosswhite is a good friend of hers. Naturally she is upset at the thought of losing her."

"I would think you would have used better judgment in choosing your daughter's friends, Emery."

"I can think of nothing against Martha," Lydia said. "She is everything we could want in a friend for our daughter."

Papa quickly said, "Perhaps we ought to change what appears to be a sensitive subject. I understand, Milton, that now there is little chance of Marshall becoming the state capitol."

I stopped listening and ran to the window. Our house is a story-and-a-half with the bedrooms squished under the roof. In front of our house are four white columns. About half the houses in Marshall, even small cottages, have white columns across the front. That's the way the ancient Greeks built their houses.

In our living room we have a picture of the Greek acropolis.

I threw on my jacket and climbed out onto one of the columns. I shinnied down to the porch wondering if the Greeks had columns on their houses for quick get aways. Through the windows I could see that everyone was still sitting around the table. They looked so safe. Not like the Crosswhites.

It was dark with no moon. Overhead it was as if someone had scattered handfuls of stars every which way across the sky. The big dipper pointed to the north star and I remembered how the Crosswhites had followed the north star to freedom. I began to run. The rain had frozen into ice and twice my legs went out from under me. In the dark, the shadows of the tree trunks looked like giant men, and the branches, like arms about to snatch me. I began to understand what it must feel like to have slave catchers after you.

At the Crosswhite's house all the lights were on. The house was crowded with the Negroes who lived nearby. Even though he didn't have on his uniform with the brass buttons I recognized Mr. Jacobs from the Marshall house.

I had heard talk as I walked through the door. Now everyone was silent, staring at me. Martha and the rest of the children were all up and dressed. They were gathered around their mother. The younger ones were hanging on as if they were afraid their mother and father would be taken from them. Mrs. Crosswhite had her baby in her arms, holding on tight.

After a long minute, Mr. Crosswhite came over and said, "You look cold, child. Come by the fire." He looked hard at me. "Does your daddy know you came here?"

Mr. Crosswhite had a way of looking at you that said, "Don't bother me with anything but the truth." I couldn't lie. I shook my head and said, "No, sir. I only came here to tell you that Lydia and Papa think there are slave catchers after you."

He frowned at me. "We thank you for thinking of us. We are just giving thought to what to do about that. I pray the Lord it isn't what we fear. We have no wish to leave our home here."

Just then Papa came into the house. "I thought I would find you here, Hilda."

Mr. Crosswhite told Daddy, "It was a kindness in her to try to warn us, Dr. Lovett."

Papa did not seem angry with me, only worried. "Hilda has let me know what Martha's suspicions were. I can tell you, Mr. Crosswhite, that Marshall will not let those men drag your family back into slavery. If they try, you must let us know at once so that we can act. It would be best if we set a signal of some kind." He looked around the room. Moses Patterson, the town crier was there. He often rode through the town ringing a bell to announce a special event like an auction sale. "Moses can give the signal," Papa said. "We'll all be listening. Now, Hilda, come along with me."

I looked at Martha. "Will I see you in school tomorrow?" I asked.

Mrs. Crosswhite said, "I expect not, Hilda. I believe I will keep the children by me tomorrow." She held her baby more closely.

## CHAPTER 5

When we got home Papa ordered me to bed. "I know you meant well, Hilda, but now you must leave things to me." As I started up the steps I heard Papa tell Lydia he was going to see the banker, General Gorham, "and some other men. Men I can depend upon."

All I could think about was Martha. What would it be like to have someone hunting you down like an animal.

I did not think I would close my eyes that night but I was tired from my hurried trip to the Crosswhites. Something else. The way you can't hear snow when it falls always puts me to sleep.

I dreamt of a house with nobody in it. A shutter slammed against an empty window making a loud sound. I jumped awake. Someone was pounding on our front door. From my window I could see the sky was just starting to lighten. In the distance I heard Moses Patterson's bell. I tumbled out of bed and ran to the landing. Lydia was downstairs in her nightdress and a wrapper, her long hair undone. Papa was buttoning his collar and reaching for his hat. As he went out the door he called over his shoulder, "You stay here, Lydia. Things may get nasty." Then he was gone.

I was down the stairs in a second. "What is it?"

Lydia put her arms around me. "General Gorham came to tell Papa that there is trouble at the Crosswhites. Papa is going to see if he can help."

"We can't just stay here!"

Lydia looked at me. "No, Hilda, I don't believe we can. I don't know what we can do there, but at least we will be a witness. That is something."

"What do you mean, 'a witness'?"

"I mean someone who sees and remembers for as long as they live. So that other people will remember to tell the story. And it will never be forgotten. Dress warmly. It's cold out. Quickly now."

Outside the darkness was leaving and the trees and houses were becoming themselves. We saw that we were not alone. It was the most amazing sight. As we hastened toward the Crosswhites we saw lights go on one by one in the houses. Front doors swung open. People pulled on their coats, clamped hats upon their heads, and rushed out of their houses. All over town people were making their way toward the Crosswhite house. Some hurried along in the cold night all by themselves. A few carried torches to light the dark-ness. Some clustered together in little groups. No one spoke. No one had to. They were all thinking the same thing. Many of our neighbors were there. Dr. Comstock was among them and Mr. Easterly, Mr. Ingersoll and Mr. Cook. All hurrying.

When we reached the Crosswhites' the Negro families who lived nearby had already gathered out-side of the house. They were talking excitedly to one another. Some were shouting. Others were angrily shaking their fists.

Through the open door we could see Papa and General Gorham. Lydia and I inched our way through the crowd to join them.

Inside the house the Crosswhites were clinging to one another. With them was the deputy sheriff, Harvey Dickson, accompanied by the two men we had seen outside of the hotel.

Papa was surprised to find us there but all he said was, "Lydia, see if you can be of help to Mrs. Crosswhite."

Martha ran to me. She pointed to the man in the corduroy jacket and whispered in my ear, "That's Mr. Troutman. He's grandson to our first master. The other man is Mr. Giltner, kin to the man who owned us. They mean to take us back to Kentucky and they got the sheriff with them. They say we can't even get our clothes together. They just put us in a wagon and take us to the law. Then south. We'll never get free again." Mrs. Crosswhite was weeping. "What will I do with my baby?" she said to Lydia. "It would break my heart to leave it but it was born here, a free child. If I take it back south it will live a slave."

"What does your mother mean?" I asked Martha.

"If a child is born in a free state like Michigan it's free for all its life. Unless it gets taken back."

"What should your mother do?"

Martha shook her head. "I don't think a baby wants to be without a mama. But I don't think a baby wants to be a slave."

Lydia said, "How can a mother make such a cruel choice?"

The sheriff and Mr. Troutman began to push the Crosswhites out the door. General Gorham was pulling them back.

"Got them out of here quick," Mr. Giltner shouted to the sheriff. "There's a crowd gathering out there."

And there was. There must have been two hundred people from the town and they were angry. There were men shaking sticks. Through the open door we could hear them shouting threats, "Leave those people alone!" "Get out of town!" "Go back where you came from!"

Mr. Troutman started to draw his gun. The sheriff, who was looking worried, put his hand on Mr.

Troutman's shoulder to stop him. "No need for that," he said. "There's a lot more of them than there is of us."

Mr. Troutman heeded the sheriff and took his hand off of his gun. He called out to the crowd. "Now you listen to me. I'm a lawyer and I know the law. I am an agent of Francis Giltner of Carroll county, Kentucky. This man here is David Giltner, his son. I ask that I be permitted peaceably to take the family of Crosswhite before a justice that I may prove they are slaves and return them to Kentucky." He was answered by more angry shouts.

General Gorham called out to him, "You have come here after some of Marshall's citizens and you cannot have them. You cannot take them by moral, physical or legal force. The quicker you leave this house, the better for you."

The shouts grew louder. General Gorham said, "I ask you for your own safety to leave  You can see how angry the crowd is."

Suddenly one of the town lawyers pushed his way through the crowd and ran up to the door waving a paper under Mr. Troutman's nose. "I have a warrant for your arrest for housebreaking and kidnapping," he said.

Mr. Troutman was taken aback. "This is an out-rage! I'll get my uncle's rightful property or I'll bring a regiment of soldiers up here from Kentucky! The

law is on my side. I'll have all of you in court. See if I don't." He began to take the names of those who were opposing him. All cheerfully gave their names.

"Charles T. Gorham," General Gorham said. "Put it down in capital letters."

"Emery A. Lovett," Papa said. "That's with two t's."

"Charles Cromwell Comstock, Jr.," Dr. Comstock said. "Put down the junior so as not to confuse me with my father."

When these remarks were reported to the crowd people began to laugh and cheer.

Mr. Troutman and the men with him looked about them as if they expected someone to come to their aid. No one did. Instead the crowd was even more determined. The sheriff spoke to Mr. Troutman in a low voice. At first Mr. Troutman shook his head. The other man with Mr. Troutman appeared to agree with the sheriff. With the sheriff leading the way the men left the house. Mr. Troutman grudgingly.

They made their way hastily through the jeering crowd and sprinted onto the wagon they had brought to take away the Crosswhites. In a moment they were out of sight.

The crowd began to cheer and clap one another on the back. Just as they had come, in small groups and one by one, the crowd left.

## CHAPTER 6

Mr. Crosswhite said, "They'll be back. I know them. They want to get their hands on us and they have the law on their side."

"We must find a way for you to get to Canada," Papa said. "They can't touch you there."

Mr. Crosswhite squared his shoulders. "I had thought to make Marshall my home. I'm all the more wanting to after how the town stood up for us tonight. But those slave catchers, they have the law on their side. They'll hunt me down if I stay in this country. Freedom comes first with me. We have to leave here for Canada. Tonight. I brought my family to freedom once and I'll do it again."

Lydia said, "I can promise you, Mr. Crosswhite, the day is coming when the people in this country will get up on their hind feet and change the law. If it takes a fight to do it, they'll fight."

If Mr. Troutman were there Lydia would have shaken him into jelly.

"I believe you Mrs. Lovett, and I'm the last man to want to break the law," General Gorham said, "but until that time comes we must do what we can for this family. If there is to be punishment for breaking the law we will take the consequences." He looked around the room. "Someone must hire a wagon to take the Crosswhites away. There is no time to lose."

Isaac Jacobs spoke up, "As hostler at the Marshall House I can hire me a wagon and a two horse team, Adam. I do it all the time so no one will know who I'm doing it for."

"I have money put by," Mr. Crosswhite said. "Whatever freedom for my family costs me, I'll pay. But where will the wagon take us? They'll be looking for us on all the roads to Detroit."

"On the roads, yes," George Ingersoll said, "but perhaps not on the train. But we must find a way to board it before it gets to Marshall. They'll be watching for you here." Mr. Ingersoll was a tall man and standing with his top hat on nearly touched the ceiling of the small house. "You can spend today in the attic of my mill. No one will think of looking for you there. When it's dark tonight I'll drive you to Battle Creek. We'll get on the train there first thing tomorrow morning. You'll be in Detroit by afternoon."

"What about the conductor on the train?" Papa asked. "He'll be taking tickets."

"It's Henry Tillotson. I know him," Mr. Ingersoll said. "He's a Marshall man. I think we can trust him. Anyhow, I'm afraid we have no other choice. Now we must be quick. They could come back and they'll have more law men with them."

The Crosswhites only had time to gather together a few clothes. It was terrible to me to see what the Crosswhites had to leave behind. The chairs Mr. Crosswhite had fashioned could not go. Neither could the rugs or the curtains Mrs. Crosswhite had made. The Crosswhites began to give all their things away to their friends.

Martha snatched up her bathing dress. "There's sure to be swimming water in Canada. I'm going to take this." Martha picked up her book of leaves. "I guess it's not going to be my town anymore," she said. She handed the book to me. We threw our arms around one another and cried. Then Mr. Ingersoll hurried the Crosswhites into his wagon and drove them away.

## CHAPTER 7

When we got back home Papa was worried. "I know the Crosswhites are just about out of medicine for their baby. Who knows when they'll be able to find more on the dangerous trip ahead of them? And it's important that the child have it."

"How will we get medicine to them?" Lydia asked. "They'll be watching everyone they saw in the Crosswhite's house this morning. If they follow you or me to Mr. Ingersoll's mill we would lead them right to the Crosswhites."

"We must find someone to send, someone they wouldn't suspect."

"Let me take it Papa." Another chance to see Martha.

"But you were there as well," Lydia said.

"But they won't suspect someone as young as me. Besides, I know how to lose anyone who follows me."

Papa gave me one of his serious looks. "There may be some truth in what you say, Hilda."

# FRIENDS

That afternoon I slipped out of our back door. Without touching it I could feel the bottle of medicine tucked down in my pocket. I was carrying my ice skates and trying to look as though I was on my way to the mill pond to skate. A little way from the pond was Mr. Ingersoll's flour mill.

It was winter crisp out like biting into an apple. The snow squeaked when you walked on it. But I wasn't cold. I was wearing two of everything. A stocking cap inside my stocking hat. Mittens inside my mittens. A sweater under my sweater and a coat under my coat. I could hardly move. The extra things were for Martha. I was sure Canada was a cold country.

The mill pond was about a mile from our house and right through town. I was hoping I would see some friends I could walk with so I wouldn't be noticed. But there was no one in sight. I was careful to keep away from the Marshall House. I made myself walk slowly as though I had all the time in the world. Even though it felt as though there was someone following me, I didn't look around.

It seemed to take forever but I finally got to the mill pond. Several of my friends were there and called to me. I sat down and put on my skates. I had so many clothes on I could hardly bend to tie them.

Everyone wanted to talk about what had happened that morning at the Crosswhites. Many of the skaters' parents had been there. "What will the Crosswhites do now?" Tom Markham asked.

Martha had once said to him, "I never know a person to have so many questions." Tom was in our class. He had grown about five inches since the beginning of the semester. I always forgot to look up high enough for him.

I started to answer when I saw something that froze my heart, a man standing at the edge of the pond. It was Mr. Troutman. He had bought a new winter jacket and hat so it had taken me a minute to recognize him. He was staring right at me. If I started off for the mill, which was just around the bend from the pond, it would give the Crosswhites away.

I grabbed at Tom's arm to make him skate along with me. He's not too interested in skating with girls so he tried to pull away. "Listen," I whispered, hanging on to him. "Don't look now but that man up there is the man that's trying to catch the Crosswhites. He's watching me. I've got to get to the Crosswhites without his noticing.  They're in the mill."

Tom looked out of the corner of his eye at me. It was a respectful look, a look I had never before had from him. "How are you going to do it?" he wanted to know.

"We're going to play crack the whip. First you'll be on the end then some other kids then me. Each time we skate closer to the mill. And tell everyone to take their time coming back. You pass the word along." With that I pushed off trying to look as if I were just practicing skating backwards.

Tom skated next to Augusta who skated next to Herman who skated next to Rosemary. They all passed the word. One by one we lined up for crack the whip. Tom was at the end. We skated around and around to pick up momentum. When we were going really fast we let go of Tom and he shot across the ice in the direction of the mill. We did it again and again. Each time with a different person at the end of the whip. Each time inching closer to the mill. When it was Rosemary's turn we couldn't even see her as she was sent gliding around the bend. It was a couple of minutes before she was back.

Then it was my turn. I had never been on the end of a game of crack the whip. I had never wanted to be. We went faster and faster. I could hardly hang on. "Let go!" Someone said. But I was too scared. Around we went. Even faster. I knew I had to let go. Dizzy as I was I could see Mr. Troutman still standing on the bank watching us. I let go.

It was like being shot out of a cannon. I slid, I flew. I was going so fast I couldn't breathe. I was around the bend. When I finally slowed down I skated as fast as I could to the mill. Looking up I saw Martha's face in the attic window. I made wild motions to her to come down. A minute later she was there, a shawl thrown over her shoulders. I gave her the medicine and the extra coat and hat and mittens. "I wish you didn't have to go away," I said.

Martha's voice was angry. "I don't want to go away. How come we got to give up so much and work so hard for something you got for free?"

"It's not fair to blame me," I said. "We've always been friends. Look at all the people who were out there this morning. They were your friends, too."

"But there's plenty of Mr. Troutmans and Mr. Giltners. What about them?"

I didn't know what to answer. "Mr. Troutman's watching," I gasped. "I've got to get back."

"I'll write to you," she said. I hugged her. As quickly as I could I skated toward the others just in time to get in line for the next crack the whip. Mr. Troutman was still there watching us. He was swinging his arms and stamping his feet to keep warm. The next time I looked he was gone.

That night Mr. Ingersoll was to carry the Crosswhites in his wagon to Battle Creek, Michigan, where in the morning they were to get on the train. The train would be passing through Marshall on its way to Detroit.

# FRIENDS

I was at the railroad station the next morning waiting for the train to come through. I knew that Martha and her family would not show themselves at the Marshall station. Still I wanted to be there. If the Crosswhites were on the train, they would be safe. Yet I was afraid if they were on the train I would never see Martha again.

A few people were standing at the station with their luggage waiting to board. I crouched down behind some trees so I could see the train but no one could see me. I was listening so hard I heard the train coming from a long distance. As it chugged into the station I looked for a sign of Martha. There was nothing to see.

The passengers boarded the train. The wagons that had brought them to the station drove off. The train began the heavy breathing that meant it was ready to go. Mr. Troutman was nowhere in sight so I moved out from behind the trees. There was Mr. Ingersoll looking out of the train window. When he saw me he tipped his tall hat and smiled at me. I knew the Crosswhites were safe. For just a minute I thought of jumping onto the train but without a ticket I knew I would soon be thrown off. I waved hard just in case Martha was watching.

## CHAPTER 8

Two days after the Crosswhites escaped Mr. Troutman was taken before Marshall's Justice of the Peace. The whole town crowded into the courtroom. Papa and Lydia and me as well. This time the crowd was joking and laughing.

Justice Van Arman accused Mr. Troutman of making a cowardly attack upon the Crosswhites. Angrily he told them, "You appeared like thieves in the night!" He made a fine speech about the "curse of slavery, and the gifts of freedom." Everyone in the courtroom stamped and cheered. "Mr. Troutman," he said, "You wanted to tear Mrs. Crosswhite from her baby!" At that we all booed and jeered. When Mr. Troutman was fined $100 the cheers were louder than ever.

Mr. Troutman came rushing out of the courtroom like he had been stung by a swarm of bees. He headed fast for the Marshall House, picked up his things and with Mr. Giltner took off for Kentucky. We thought never to see him again but that wasn't so.

# FRIENDS

What he did when he got back to his home was to tell everybody in the State of Kentucky how he was set upon and knocked about by the citizens of Marshall, Michigan. He meant to have revenge on us. The state of Kentucky rose up and sent a nasty letter to the state of Michigan. And that wasn't all. There was to be a court trial in Detroit brought by Mr. Troutman and Mr. Giltner against General Gorham, Dr. Comstock, Papa and several of the other men who had protected the Crosswhites. They were accused under the Fugitive Slave Law which says it's a crime to harbor a slave or to assist a slave in running away.

"Will you go to jail, Papa?" I asked, blinking to keep my tears back.

"It isn't a question of jail, Hilda. Mr. Troutman is suing us for a great deal of money. So much money it would ruin us. What's more we will have to hire lawyers and go to Detroit for the trial. But whatever it costs we are resolved to fight Troutman for we know what we did was right."

At first only Lydia was going to accompany Papa to Detroit. I begged to go as well. Even though he said he wasn't going to jail I didn't want to let papa out of my sight.

"Let her come, Emery," Lydia said. "What better chance will she have to hear justice argued."

# FRIENDS

We traveled by the same train that Martha took. Our tickets cost $2.50. It was my first train ride. I had to hold my breath the houses and fields went by so fast. It seemed no time at all before the train pulled right into the middle of Detroit. A city of fifteen thousand people! You could hardly cross a street for carriages and wagons dashing by.

We stayed right in the middle of Detroit at the Woodworth's Hotel. It had an elegant dining room but we didn't eat there for it was expensive. Lydia had packed a hamper of food which we ate in our room, careful not to get crumbs on the fine carpets. After two days the food was all gone but by then the anti-slavery society in town had heard about us and invited us for meals.

It was at one of these houses, the house of the DeBaptistes, a Negro family who lived on Beaubien Street, that I finally heard what had happened to the Crosswhites. Mr. DeBaptiste had once been the steward of President Harrison. Now he was a business man who owned his own steamboat. Only Negroes were not permitted to have a license to pilot boats so he had to hire a white man to be the captain of his boat.

Mr. DeBaptiste told us that after the train had carried the Crosswhites to Detroit they were brought to the Second Baptist church. The church was started by escaped slaves. For ten years the church members had helped other slaves to escape by hiding them in the church basement or taking them into their own homes. So many slaves ran away to the city of Detroit, the city even had its own secret name. It was called "Midnight" by escaping slaves.

The Crosswhites had been hidden in the basement of the church. On Sunday morning the minister had preached a sermon with special words tucked into it. The words were a signal to the people in the congregation that help was needed for a family.

After dark that night someone in the congregation brought a wagon with a secret compartment to carry the Crosswhites to the foot of Woodward Avenue where someone else had a barge waiting. The Crosswhites had crossed the Detroit River to Canada and freedom.

I begged Lydia and Papa to show me the church where Martha had been hidden. Like the DeBaptiste's house, the church was on Beaubien Street and had once been a schoolhouse. Afterwards we went to see the place where Martha and her family had crossed the river.

Standing on the shore you could look right across the river and actually see Canada. Canada didn't look so different from America. It was difficult to believe it was another country altogether. I stared hard hoping to see Martha but I knew I was being foolish. By now Martha would be far away.

The river was crowded with paddle-wheelers and schooners and sloops and steamships. Papa said the steamship, *Michigan*, was 156 feet long! About the size of the Marshall courthouse! There were boats loaded with lumber. There were boats loaded with salt from the nearby salt mines. And there were passenger boats. People came every day from across the ocean to New York. From New York they sailed up the Hudson River through the Erie Canal and into Lake Erie. As you walked the streets of Detroit you heard many languages. And the stores! How I looked into the windows of the fine Manhattan Store with hats such as I had never imagined. How I wished Martha were with me.

One night we dined with Mr. Zachariah Chandler who had helped the Crosswhites in their escape to Canada. He owned a large dry goods store and lived in a great stone house on Second and Fort street, a street of elegant homes. His house had a kind of porch you could drive your carriage under so you wouldn't get wet.

Mr. Chandler was a big man with red hair and an Irish brogue. Though he had a rough manner, he was kindness itself. Lydia told me during Detroit's cholera epidemic he had served as a nurse to the dying.

# FRIENDS

His roughness came only when he spoke of slavery. He called it 'the great national wrong.'

"I'll fight it wherever I find it," he said, thrusting out his pugnacious jaw. "I'll fight anyone who doesn't fight against it. And one day the free states will rise up and fight."

"Do you think we'll have a chance to win the trial?" Papa asked him at dinner.

"If we don't win against the forces of slavery this time," Mr. Chandler said, "we will win the next time. And if not the next time the time after that. All that is needed is that we keep fighting." He thrust out his great jaw and squared his shoulders and grasped his knife and fork like weapons. I believe at that moment he would have attacked any slave catcher who walked through the door and eaten him up.

The day of the trial Lydia and I went with Papa to the federal courthouse. The courtroom was filled. Lydia and I just managed to get two seats before the doors were closed. The courtroom was very solemn. All the lawyers and the men on trial were dressed up in suits. When Judge McLean came into the room we all had to stand up. He was wearing a long black gown and a stern look which made him a little scary. What was most impressive was that he was a judge of the Supreme Court of the United States and had come all the way from Washington to hear the trial.

# FRIENDS

It was like two teams fighting one another. Papa and General Gorham and Dr. Comstock and the other men were sitting with their lawyer at one table. Mr. Troutman and Mr. Giltner were sitting at another table with their lawyer. Lydia explained that each side would get a chance to tell their story. Mr. Troutman and Mr. Giltner's side would start first.

Before anyone could speak they had to promise to tell the truth. Mr. Giltner said, "The Crosswhites are the slaves owned by my father. They ran away but they are still my father's property. He asked Mr. Troutman and me to bring them back."

When he called the Crosswhites 'property' there were a lot of angry mumbles in the courtroom and the judge had to pound with his hammer, 'gavel,' Lydia called it, to make the courtroom quiet.

Mr. Troutman got up and promised to tell the truth. His lawyer asked, "What were you doing the morning of January 27 at the home of Adam Crosswhite?"

Mr. Troutman cleared his throat. He looked a little nervous. He knew he didn't have many friends in that courtroom.

"I was there to take the Crosswhites before a Justice and prove that they were the property of Mr. Giltner. I would then return the Crosswhites to him. He is their rightful owner."

"And why did you not carry out your plan?"

"There was an angry mob outside who prevented me."

"Can you name any members of that mob?"

"Indeed I can." Mr. Troutman pointed to General Gorham and Dr. Comstock and Papa and several of the others, calling out their names.

"How did these men prevent you from taking the Crosswhites?"

Mr. Troutman looked right at General Gorham. "General Gorham said, "You cannot take them by moral, physical or legal force."

"In other words, General Gorham refused to let you take the Crosswhites?"

"That is correct."

"Do you recall the conversation?"

"Yes. General Gorham said, 'What are you doing here?' I answered, 'I have come to take the slaves who belong to Mr. Giltner.' General Gorham said, 'You can't take them.'"

Then witnesses were put upon the stand to say that Mr. Troutman had remained a gentleman in spite of the crowd not letting him do what he wished. He had not hit anyone or killed anyone.

Next it was the turn of General Gorham and Papa and rest of the men.

General Gorham promised to tell the truth and went upon the stand. His lawyer asked him if he remembered what he said to Mr. Troutman.

"I do. I asked, 'What are you doing here?' Troutman answered, 'I have come to take the slaves who belong to Mr. Giltner.' I said, 'You can't take them.' Mr. Troutman said, 'Do you say I can't?' I said, 'I said no such thing. I am just pointing out to you that the crowd is very angry and it would be dangerous for you to try to take them.'"

The lawyer smiled. "In other words you were not hindering him from taking the Crosswhites, you were merely protecting him from the anger of the crowd."

"That is correct."

Mr. Troutman's lawyer got after General Gorham. He asked, "Did you not say, sir, 'We will not allow our citizens to be kidnapped and taken back to slavery?' And did you not further say, 'The dear people are the law and you can't have the Negroes?'"

General Gorham was getting angry and answered, "I was there to prevent violence and to preserve the peace. I did nothing to excite the crowd, but I will not hide the fact that I despise slavery and those who practice it."

At that there was a loud cheer in the courtroom and the judge had to bang his hammer again and again until I thought it would fly apart.

One good thing happened. Mr. Troutman did not have enough proof that Papa or any of the other men had hindered him. Only General Gorham. So Papa and the other men were let off. But General Gorham's trial continued for several days and we worried for him. We came every day and watched the jury. We tried to guess how they would decide. One day we thought one thing, the next, another thing.

The lawyers for each side got a chance to present their sides. General Gorham's lawyer said, "Your Honor and members of the jury, in all of the ten years that Michigan has been a state it has been a free state. It stands for freedom for all its citizens. These men," here he pointed to Mr. Troutman and Mr. Giltner, "came to tear this mother and father and their innocent children away from their home, their work and their friends. General Gorham did not cause this crowd to gather. These people came of their own accord. They came out of the goodness of their hearts to protect one of their neighbors. It was General Gorham's purpose to prevent violence and preserve peace. He did nothing to excite the crowd. They were friends of the Crosswhites and friends of freedom. You cannot punish a man for standing up for freedom and justice."

Mr. Troutman's lawyer took off his jacket and hitched up his suspenders. "Your Honor and members of the jury, however unjust you may believe slavery to be, the people of Kentucky have adopted it.

# FRIENDS

Our Constitution and the Fugitive Slave Act are the law of the United States of America. You are sworn to uphold the law and you must do so."

Then it was the judge's turn. His glasses had slipped to the end of his nose. He looked sternly over his glasses at us to let us know if we said anything there would be lots of hammering. We all held our breath. The judge turned to the jury. "From the evidence, it seems that many of the most orderly and respectable citizens of Marshall were found at the house of the Crosswhites. And so far as they may have been there to protect the rights of the Crosswhites from an illegal seizure, they are not to be condemned. But after they were told by Mr. Troutman that he was taking the Crosswhites before a justice to prove that they were Mr. Giltner's slaves, there was no excuse for opposing him." The judge pushed his glasses up on his nose and said in a grave voice, "That man is a dangerous citizen who follows his conscience in violation of the legal rights of others."

The judge cleared his throat. "The law is clear," he said. He looked very serious and not very happy. "Anyone who hinders, harbors, or conceals a person after notice that the person was a fugitive from labor shall pay a fine."

After that I did not have much hope. I hung on to Lydia's hand. When the jury came in General Gorham was declared guilty. He was fined the cost of the Crosswhite family. Five hundred dollars for each member of the family and the cost of the trial. Nearly four thousand dollars! A huge sum of money! Even though General Gorham was pretty well off it was a lot more money than he had.

Dr. Comstock and Papa and the other men hurried to General Gorham's side to see how they might put their money together and help him. As they were talking, Zachariah Chandler strode up and handed General Gorham a check for the whole amount. He said, "It is a privilege to make my small contribution to what has been an act of courage by the citizens of Marshall."

I hadn't been able to keep from crying when I heard the jury's verdict. I told Lydia, "They put a price on each one of the Crosswhites. Like you could buy and sell Martha. It's not fair."

Lydia tried to comfort me. "Hilda, I feel as badly as you do. Only remember that people all over the country are hearing about families like the Crosswhites. There are thousands upon thousands of citizens out there opposed to slavery."

"But what good is feeling bad? It doesn't stop slavery."

"It's not just Marshall. People everywhere are fighting slavery. By the time you are a young woman, slavery will be gone from this country."

That was years away and Martha would be a grown woman as well.

There was a great crowd at the railroad station to welcome us back to Marshall. In no time the town went back to business as usual. But I could not forget Martha. I wondered if I would ever hear from her. I wondered where she was. On the map Canada seemed huge.

## CHAPTER 9

*September 10, 1850*

*Dear Hilda,*

*We're free for sure. There's no slavery allowed in Canada. And it's not so cold here as I thought it would be. There are maple and oak trees and fields of wheat and corn just like Marshall. There's a river here, too. But not so big as the Kalamazoo. When we first got here we moved in with a family. Now Daddy has work and we have a little house to ourselves. Mama and me had a garden to tend this summer. Nearby are blackberries.*

*A day's ride from here you can get right to the edge of Canada. You can see across the St. Clair River. And there is America. It doesn't look so far. But we can't go. Daddy says, "Someday.*

*Your friend,*

*Martha Crosswhite*

# FRIENDS

*October 15, 1850*

*Dear Martha,*

*I was so happy to receive your letter and know you are safe. Just last week a family like yours arrived in Marshall from the south. It is much harder to escape now because of the new Fugitive Slave Law. If you help slaves they don't just fine you. They can put you in jail! Everyone here hates the new law. Lydia wants to go to Washington and box the ears of the congressmen. Papa won't let her.*

*Mr. Chandler who helped you to escape is now the mayor of Detroit. Some say he will be a senator one day and will help in the fight against slavery.*

*I read your letter to Tom Markham. He says to say hello. I help him with his arithmetic. After school we stop by his father's daguerreotype shop. If I ever get my picture taken I'll send it to you.*

*I'm enclosing some leaves. They are just turning red and gold here in Marshall.*

*Your friend,*

*Hilda Lovett*

# FRIENDS

*November 2, 1857*

*Dear Hilda,*

*Do you remember me? It's been many years since I wrote to you. I can hardly believe we are grown women. I often think about Marshall. Does your stepmother still make that good shortbread?*

*I am writing to let you know I am getting married. I am marrying Luke Witridge. It seems right to tell you. I know many people here but you were my first friend.*

*Luke came up from Kentucky like our family did. He is a fine carpenter and he is going to build us a house. He says maybe he'll put a couple of columns on the front of it. I told him about your house. Papa still talks about Marshall and says one day he is going back. People are kind here but I often think of the good times we had in Marshall. Do they still swim in the mill pond? I kept my swimming dress.*

*Your friend,*

*Martha Crosswhite*

# FRIENDS

*December 30, 1858*

*Dear Martha,*

*What a wonderful surprise your letter was! I, too, have news! Tom Markham and I were married last month. Tom is a reporter for the* Statesman. *I am sending you an article he wrote about the Dred Scott decision made by the Supreme Court. Mr. Dred Scott was an escaped slave. He tried to make the courts give him his freedom. The Supreme Court said a slave or a descendant of slaves could not be a citizen of the United States. So Mr. Scott has no right to ask the court for freedom. Did you ever hear anything so stupid?*

*Judge McLean disagreed with that decision. He was the judge in the trial against General Gorham in Detroit. What happened to your family must have stayed in his mind for he wrote down how he thought the Dred Scott decision was a bad ruling.*

*As you can see by Tom's article we are all angry with the Supreme Court. How can they be so wrong! Everyone here is so mad they are ready to go to war.*

*Your friend,*

*Hilda Markham*

# FRIENDS

*November 30, 1861*

*Dear Hilda,*

*I am so worried. Luke has left Canada to return to America. He is going to be a soldier. I didn't want him to go but he said we could never live in America until the war is won. It scares me that he might have to go back to Kentucky and fight. What would happen if they caught him?*

*I and my son, James, have moved in with Daddy and Mama. All their children except the youngest are grown so there is plenty of room. Daddy says if he were younger he would march off with Luke.*

*Your friend,*

*Martha Witridge*

# FRIENDS

*March 19, 1862*

*Dear Martha,*

*Tom is fighting in the war, too. We have great faith here in President Lincoln. Papa has gone to be a doctor and Lydia went with him to nurse the soldiers. I care for my two girls, Elizabeth and Emily, and do all I can for the soldiers. The sheets from my hope chest have all been torn into bandages. It seems like I have knitted enough socks for a dozen armies. I only pray Luke and Tom will never need the bandages and won't have to wear my ugly socks. Miss Growling would never approve of the way I turn my heels.*

*Your friend,*

*Hilda Markham*

# FRIENDS

*December 13, 1866*

*Dear Hilda,*

*Luke is back, thin as a stick but safe. Many of his friends were lost in the war. He cannot talk about the fighting without tears coming into his eyes. I know there is much he doesn't tell me.*

*Luke says he wants to live in the country he fought for. Daddy and Mama want to go home. We're coming back to Marshall.*

*Your friend,*

*Martha Witridge*

FRIENDS

## AUTHOR'S NOTE

Much of this story is true. The Crosswhite family escaped slavery in Kentucky to settle in Marshall, Michigan. When Mr. Troutman and Mr. Giltner tried to return them to Kentucky the whole town of Marshall came out to protect the Crosswhites. General Gorham, George Ingersoll, Isaac Jacobs and many of the other citizens of Marshall I have mentioned were there that morning. They helped in the Crosswhite's escape to Canada.

In Marshall, Michigan you will find a marker near the site of the Crosswhite cabin. In the Marshall library there is a collection of articles that tell the story of the Crosswhites. The State of Michigan law books record the trial of *Troutman vs. Gorham*, presided over by Supreme Court Justice McLean. Zachariah Chandler, who was to become a United States Senator and a Secretary of the Interior, paid General Gorham's fine.

It is believed that at the war's end some members of the Crosswhite family returned to Marshall. The names and ages of the Crosswhite's children are not known and Hilda Lovett and her family are imagined.

The courage of the citizens of Marshall is real.